Alaska's Snow White

and Her Seven Sled Dogs

Written and Illustrated by

Mindy Dwyer

little bigfoot

an imprint of sasquatch books
seattle, wa

For Katey, my self-rescuing Alaskan princess
and Ruby, her trusty sled dog

"As long as you live and breathe, believe. Believe for those who
cannot. Believe even if you stopped believing. Believe for the sake
of the dead, for love, to keep your heart beating, believe. Never
give up, never despair, let no mystery confound you into the
conclusion that mystery cannot be yours."
—MARK HELPRIN, *A Soldier of the Great War*

Manufactured in China by Midas Printing International Ltd.
(Hong Kong), in October 2014

Published by Little Bigfoot, an imprint of Sasquatch Books

20 19 18 17 16 15   9 8 7 6 5 4 3 2 1

Editor: Tegan Tigani
Project editor: Nancy W. Cortelyou
Illustrations: Mindy Dwyer
Design: Joyce Hwang

Library of Congress Cataloging-in-Publication Data is available.

ISBN: 978-1-57061-975-5

Sasquatch Books
1904 Third Avenue, Suite 710
Seattle, WA 98101
(206) 467-4300
www.sasquatchbooks.com
custserv@sasquatchbooks.com

Once upon a time, far north at the top of the Everwinter Mountains, in a palace made of ice, a tiny princess was born.

Her mother whispered, "Your hair is as black as this winter night, your lips are redder than a salmonberry, and your skin is as white as freshly fallen snow. My fairest Snow White, you will always be loved." Then the Queen closed her eyes and died.

That winter and for several winters after, there would be no Ice Festival—no ice cream, no popsicles of every flavor, no ice carvings, no bobsled run, no kaleidoscope ice rink, and no Great Race in the grieving kingdom. But the children in the village believed that one day there would be a festival once more.

Eventually the King married again. Although the new Queen was beautiful, there was something about her that was painful to look at. The King was so enchanted with her, he did not see it, even when the mirror declared:

"You, my queen, are the fairest by far,
   And never nice is what you are."

The mirror was correct. The Queen was not nice, and she had no time for a young princess in her kingdom. She bewitched the King into sending off his only daughter to live in the village. The Master Skate Maker and his kind wife raised Snow White as their own.

One day the mirror revealed,

"My queen, this news
I hate to bear:
The princess is
now twice as fair!
With hair night-
black, and lips
berry-red,
Snow White's
beauty turns
every head.
Her skin is white
as freshly fallen
snow—She's the
fairest of all, now
this I know."

Furious with jealousy, the
Queen shouted to the Palace
Musher, "Bring me
her heart!"

He mushed down the mountain to the village. Snow White's hair was truly black as a winter's night, her lips redder than a salmonberry, and her skin as white as freshly fallen snow, but it was her extraordinary eyes that melted his heart.

He gave her his favorite dog, Blue—a trusted Husky with one blue eye and one green eye—plus three pairs from his dog team, along with a sled.

"Run away, Snow White!" he warned. "Never return, or the Queen will cut out both of our hearts!"

She ran away as fast as the dogs could go until she was deep in the wilderness.

"**Whoooo, whooo?**" asked a snowy owl from the darkness.

"It is I, Snow White."

The owl flew home to the Master Skate Maker and his wife and reassured them, "Snow White wanders, but your daughter is not lost."

Snow White chose Scout for her lead dog, saying, "Scout, you'll help me find the way!"

Ruby, her swing dog, wagged her tail when Snow White told her, "You are the smart one." And she knew Ruby's partner, Warrior, would protect them from danger.

Hunter could provide them with meat out on the trail, and his partner, Sniffy, the other team dog, had a good nose for trouble.

Her wheel dogs, Blue and Fluffy, were closest to her in the team. "Blue," she whispered, "you will keep me from getting lonely out in the wilderness." Fluffy, the mama dog, curled around her. Snow White said, "Fluffy, I know who will keep me warm."

With her seven dogs, she felt safe and ready for adventure.

The Musher returned to the palace with the heart of a mountain goat. The Queen fried it with onions, ate it, and proclaimed, "Now, I am forever the fairest of all."

But one day the mirror spoke again:

"I will not lie even if I could,
For the princess still lives. In a faraway wood,
Over seven mountains, a night and one day,
With seven loyal dogs she travels by sleigh."

The wicked Queen roared, *"I will deal with this!"* and she turned herself into a Fur Trapper. She crossed the seven mountains by sled and tracked down Snow White.

The fake Trapper and the true princess met on the trail. The Trapper held up a dazzling coat made of 777 snowshoe hares sewn with slipknots. "It is just your size. You must have it!" The Trapper wrapped the coat around Snow White, zipping up the ruff so tightly that it squeezed the breath out of her.

As the Queen dashed away, her wicked laugh sailed behind, freezing in the air and crackling into a thousand sharp ice crystals.

Snow White's loyal dog Warrior pounced
on the rabbit coat and shredded it to
pieces. When Snow White woke up, the
coat slipped from her memory completely.

A raven saw it all and flew to Snow White's
parents to tell them that she was still alive.

When the Queen next visited her mirror, it told her:

"Snow White lives, my queen,
With my own eyes I've seen!
She roams the snow with
   seven dogs and a sled,
And is even more beautiful
   now, it's said."

The Queen turned herself into a Moose Hunter
and set out on a snow machine to find the girl.
They greeted each other as folks do in the bush,
and she offered Snow White a snack of moose
jerky. It was poisoned, but Sniffy smelled the trick.
He bit the Queen on the leg and the dog pack
chased her away.

Snow White sent a dove home to her parents with
a message to let them know she was safe.

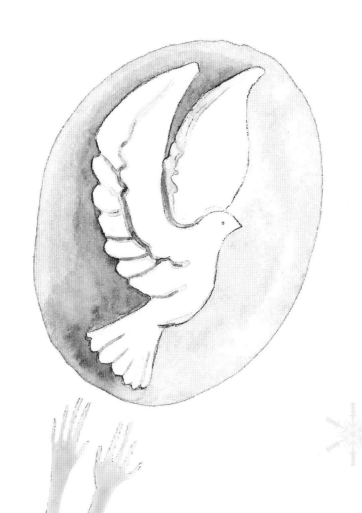

The Queen did not give up. Next, she changed herself into an Old Homesteader on snowshoes.

"Hello, my friend, may I offer you a refreshing drink?" she asked, holding up a shimmering blue bottle. Snow White was now wary of strangers and refused, even though she was thirsty after all that day's mushing.

"There is nothing to fear," said the old woman, taking a sip of the liquid ice to prove it was safe. "**See?**"

It had no effect on the wicked Queen. But, with one tiny sip of the ice-cold peppermint drink, Snow White's heart froze solid, and she fell down in the snow.

Snow White's frozen hair was as black as a winter's night, her frozen lips redder than a salmonberry, and her frozen skin whiter than freshly fallen snow. Her faithful dogs curled up in a circle around her.

Back at the palace the magic mirror announced:

"Oh, my queen, 'tis once again true,
The fairest of all can only be you."

"Yes! Bring on the Ice Festival! Let's have The Great Race!" declared the Queen. She wanted to show off her ice skating skills and be admired by all.

The Great Race was one thousand miles by sled dog. One excited young musher practiced with his dogs:

"*Hike!*" (Go!); "*Gee!*" (Right); "*Haw!*" (Left); "*Whoa!*"(Stop).

He got lost in all the excitement.

The young man, almost crazy from the cold, stumbled across a frozen young woman in the wilderness, surrounded by seven loyal and loving sled dogs. Her frozen hair was as black as a winter's night, her frozen lips redder than a salmonberry, and her frozen skin whiter than the freshly fallen snow.

It warmed his heart just to look at her. He felt a spark of love that ignited into flame and built a blazing fire. He began to melt Snow White's frozen heart. She opened her eyes and said, "I have been sent away, trapped, hunted, and tricked, and now here you are. Who are you?"

"I am Jacob, and honestly, I have no idea where I am," he said.

"Good thing I do," said Snow White. "It is time for us both to go home. Come with me.

No more was Snow White a person alone in the world;
she was the world to one person. In the icy light of dawn,
Snow White and Jacob made a tandem team of dogs and sleds. She led
the way out of the wilderness, across the seven mountains, back to the village.
The young man was smitten with her sledding skills, and she was in awe of his honesty.

The Master Skate Maker and his wife were so happy to see
Snow White. Together they hatched a plan to make a dazzling pair of skates for the
Queen to make sure she would never harm Snow White—or anyone—again. Tiny mirrors were
lovingly sewn into the leather, but superstrong magnets were hidden inside the diamond-sharp blades.

Jacob delivered the skates to the palace as the entire kingdom made ready for the Ice Festival. They polished the kaleidoscope rink, froze every flavor of ice cream and popsicle, carved massive ice sculptures, and poured hot water on the bobsled run to make it smooth and fast.

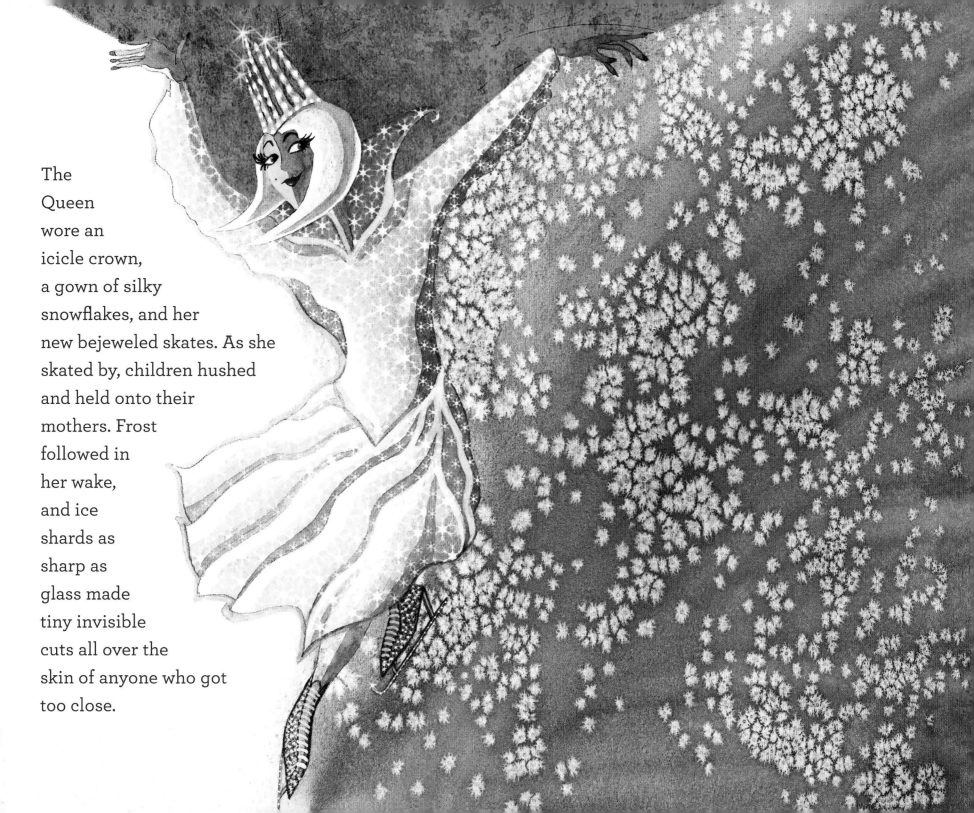

The
Queen
wore an
icicle crown,
a gown of silky
snowflakes, and her
new bejeweled skates. As she
skated by, children hushed
and held onto their
mothers. Frost
followed in
her wake,
and ice
shards as
sharp as
glass made
tiny invisible
cuts all over the
skin of anyone who got
too close.

When the Queen saw Snow White she skated faster and faster. Sparks of anger flew around and around. The magnets in her skates kept her feet moving so she couldn't stop until she carved a hole right through the ice! The terrible Queen plunged into the frigid water, and all that was left was her horrid reflection.

The villagers renamed their winter celebration The Festival of Light. Lanterns lit up the village warming the hearts of everyone. There were hot cocoas in every flavor, milk chocolate mousses, hot cakes, creamy éclairs, and gigantic chocolate carvings that you were allowed to nibble.

Snow White and Jacob, along with Scout, Ruby, Warrior, Hunter, Sniffy, Blue, and Fluffy, trained for The Great Race and won many years in a row.

The King was
never heard fro[m]
again, ar[ound th]
day, whe[n]
at the regal [mountain,]
all you see is sn[ow] and
ice. But the children of the
village believe the palace—
and the magic mirror—are
still there.